The
Other Emily

Gibbs Davis

Illustrated by Linda Shute

Houghton Mifflin Company Boston

Library of Congress Cataloging in Publication Data

Davis, Gibbs.
  The other Emily.
  Summary: Emily believes her name belongs to her alone, but on the first day of school she discovers she is not the only Emily in the world.
  ISBN 0-395-35482-X
  [1. Names, Personal—Fiction. 2. Schools—Fiction] I. Shute, Linda, ill. II. Title.
PZ7.D28860t   1984   83-18913
[E]

Printed in the United States of America

RNF ISBN 0-395-35482-X
PAP ISBN 0-395-54947-7

WOZ 10 9 8 7 6

For the one and only Emily, whose Aunt Kathryn has known and loved her from the very beginning.
— G.D.

For my one and only, Emil.
— L.M.S.

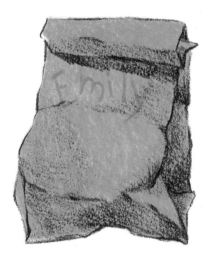

Emily loved her name. Everything about it was perfect. It wasn't too long or too short, and it started with her favorite letter — E.

Emily's father showed her how to turn the letter E on its side and make it into a Daddy Longlegs spider.

Emily's mother showed her how to turn the letter E into a comb by drawing a few extra lines.

But most of all Emily liked the letter E because it was the beginning of her name.

As soon as Emily learned how to spell her name she wrote it on her chalkboard in five different colors.

In the summer, she drew her name in the sand at the beach.

In the winter, she carved her name in the snow.

Sometimes after taking a hot steamy bath, she wrote EMILY on the bathroom window with her finger.

For her birthday, Emily's father made a special night-light with her name on it. Now, when Emily woke up in the dark she was never scared. The soft glow of her EMILY night-light reminded her she was safe in her own bedroom.

"Tomorrow is a special day," her mother said at the dinner table. Emily was busy making a big E with the peas on her plate.

"It's your first day at school," her father said. "We have a present for you."

Emily opened the box. Inside was a T-shirt with bright red letters.

"What does it say?" she asked.

"THE ONE AND ONLY EMILY," her father said.

"Gee, thanks," Emily said. She couldn't wait to wear her new present to school tomorrow.

The next morning Emily was the first one up. She put on her new T-shirt, ate breakfast, and ran outside to wait for the bus.

"You'll make lots of new friends," her mother said.

"Just walk up to someone, smile, and tell her your name," her father said.

That's easy, Emily thought, getting on the bus. I can remember that. She waved good-bye from the bus window.

Emily's classroom was sunny and had lots of plants. There was an aquarium filled with brightly colored fish.

Emily liked her teacher, Mrs. Harper. During story hour Mrs. Harper sat on a big soft couch, and Emily sat next to her. At the end of the story everyone said "The End" together. It was a perfect morning.

"Now, let's go around the room and have everyone say their name," Mrs. Harper said. "Who wants to go first?"

Emily raised her hand. She couldn't wait to say her name out loud to her new classmates.

"My name is Emily," she said. All the other children looked at her and smiled. Emily was happier than she had ever been.

"Very good, Emily," Mrs. Harper said. She nodded toward the boy sitting next to Emily.

"My name is Charlie," he whispered from behind a pillow.

"Katie," said the next little girl.

"John," said another boy.

By the time they had gotten around to the last child Emily had already forgotten most of their names.

"What's your name?" Mrs. Harper asked the last little girl.

"Emily," she said.

"That's *my* name!" Emily said.

"Yes," Mrs. Harper said. "We are lucky to have two Emilys in our class this year."

Emily didn't feel very lucky. Mrs. Harper couldn't be right. She was the one and only Emily. Emily watched the little girl closely all day. She didn't act at all like a real Emily.

"Time to get ready to go home," Mrs. Harper said.

As the children put on their sweaters and jackets Emily remembered what her father said. *Just walk up to someone, smile, and tell her your name.* Emily decided to give the other girl one more chance.

Emily walked up to her and smiled.

"Hi. I'm Emily."

"Me, too," the girl said. "My name is Emily." She turned around. EMILY was sewn on the back of her sweater in big letters.

It was true! There was *another* Emily in the
world!

"See you tomorrow," the other Emily said.

All the way home on the bus Emily felt sick. Suddenly she had a terrible thought. Maybe there were even *more* Emilys in the world. Maybe even the girl sitting next to her was named Emily.

Emily turned to her. "What's your name?"

"Debbie."

"Oh." Emily felt better. "Do you have any Emilys in your class?"

"No. Why?"

"I thought I was the one and only Emily, but there's another one in my class."

The girl laughed. "You really thought you were the *only* Emily?"

Emily felt like punching her in the nose.

"Don't feel bad," the girl said. "You're lucky your name isn't Debbie, like mine. There are Debbies in every class."

"But I thought I was the only Emily."

"You'll get used to it," the girl said.

I'll never get used to it, Emily thought as she got off the bus.

Emily stomped into the kitchen. "Somebody else has my name," she told her mother.

"Did you like her?" her mother asked.

"No! I wish she'd go away!"

Emily went out back to see her father.

"There's another Emily at my school," she said.

"That's nice."

"You told me I was the one and only Emily."

"You are the one and only Emily in our family," he said. "Lots of people share the same names. You'll get used to it."

He sounded like the girl on the bus. Nobody understood.

When she went to bed that night she looked at her EMILY night-light glowing in the dark. She didn't feel special anymore.

The next day at school was Show and Tell. Emily decided to bring the big seashell her grandmother had sent her from Florida. Emily was sure it was the only seashell like it in the world. She kept it hidden in a paper bag all day.

"Hi," said the other Emily. She was carrying a paper bag, too. "Want to know what I brought for Show and Tell?"

"No," Emily said. She stared at the other Emily and wished she would disappear.

The other Emily followed her around all day. She painted a picture next to Emily. She built a castle next to Emily and ate her crackers and milk next to Emily. She even took a nap next to Emily.

"Time for Show and Tell," Mrs. Harper said, clapping her hands together. "Everyone get your things and sit down."

Emily sat down and looked at the seashell inside her bag. She had kept her secret hidden all day.

The other Emily sat down next to her. Emily peeked inside her bag and saw something white and bumpy on the outside, pink and smooth on the inside. It was a seashell just like hers!

"You have a shell, too!" she cried.

The other Emily pulled the same shell out
of her bag. "There are shells like this all over
Florida," she said.

"How do you know?" Emily asked.

"I used to live there," she said.

Emily looked at her. She had never known
anyone who had lived someplace else.

"Can I see your shell?" the other Emily asked. Emily slowly opened her bag. "It's pretty," she said.

Emily thought the other shell was pretty too, but she didn't say anything. Then the other Emily did something strange. She cupped her shell over one ear.

"What are you doing?" Emily asked.

"Listening to the ocean," she said. "Try it."

Emily pressed her shell against her ear. The sound of ocean waves roared inside her head.

"I hear it!" Emily said. The other Emily was right. Both Emilys looked deep inside their shells for signs of the ocean.

"If we show our shells together it won't be so scary," the other Emily said.

"I will if you will," Emily said. She was glad that the other Emily had been scared, too.

"Who wants to Show and Tell next?" Mrs. Harper asked the class.

"We do," Emily said.

Both Emilys walked to the front of the class.

"We have seashells," the other Emily said.

"They're from the ocean," Emily said. "You can hear ocean sounds by holding it up to your ear like this."

Both Emilys held their shells up to their ears and listened.

"Mine roars," Emily said.

"Mine roars, too," the other Emily agreed.

They switched shells, held them tightly against their ears, and smiled at each other. It was more fun listening together than listening alone.

The class clapped for the two Emilys.

On the way home on the bus Emily looked at the seashell cradled in her lap and smiled. Tomorrow she would show the other Emily how to make a dandelion crown.